For
Kavi
&
Siva

ATHENEUM BOOKS FOR YOUNG READERS · An imprint of Simon & Schuster Children's Publishing Division · 1230 Avenue of the Americas, New York, New York 10020 · Copyright © 2011 by Calef Brown · All rights reserved, including the right of reproduction in whole or in part in any form. · ATHENEUM BOOKS FOR YOUNG READERS is a registered trademark of Simon & Schuster, Inc. · For information about special discounts for bulk purchases, please contact Simon & Schuster Special Sales at 1-866-506-1949 or business@simonandschuster.com. · The Simon & Schuster Speakers Bureau can bring authors to your live event. For more information or to book an event, contact the Simon & Schuster Speakers Bureau at 1-866-248-3049 or visit our website at www.simonspeakers.com. · Book design by Debra Sfetsios–Conover · The text for this book is set in Clearface. · The illustrations for this book are rendered in Acrylic. · Manufactured in China · 0411 SCP · First Edition · 10 9 8 7 6 5 4 3 2 1 · Library of Congress Cataloging-in-Publication Data · Brown, Calef. · Boy wonders / Calef Brown. —1st ed. · p. cm. · Summary: A young boy's questions lead to more and more questions, but there do not seem to be any answers. · ISBN 978-1-4169-7877-0 · [1. Stories in rhyme. 2. Questions and answers—Fiction. 3. Humorous stories.] I. Title. · PZ8.3.B8135Boy 2011 · [E]—dc22 · 2010020976

BOY WONDERS

CALEF BROWN

ATHENEUM BOOKS FOR YOUNG READERS
New York   London   Toronto   Sydney

May I ask you something?

Are you ever perplexed?

Completely vexed?

Do you have questions?

QUERIES?

ODD THEORIES?

Do bees get hives?

Do onions cry?

Is pepper apt to sneeze?

Do paper plates
and two-by-fours
remember being trees?

Are phones annoyed
if no one calls?

**Do ants, when anxious,
climb the walls?**

Is water scared of waterfalls?

It often makes me *wonder*. . . . .

Are baked clams okay for **clambakes** and **bake sales** alike?

If I'm too tired, am I a bike?

Is there any truth to the old myth **that gargoyles use garlic oils to gargle with?**

If I ever encounter mosquitos
**the size of chickens,
should I run like the DICKENS?**

Or would it be a better bet
**to find some chicken wire
and make a mosquito net?**

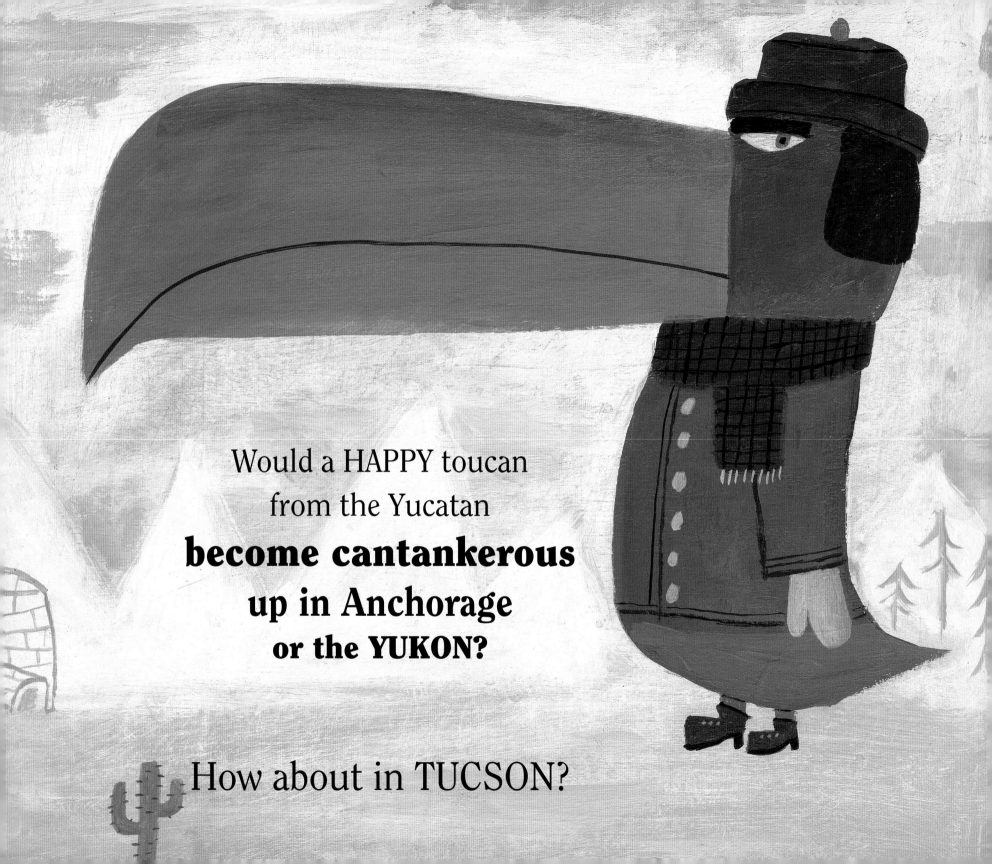

Would a HAPPY toucan
from the Yucatan
**become cantankerous
up in Anchorage
or the YUKON?**

How about in TUCSON?

Are **lazy flies** on the horizon
the prize that spiders keep their **eyes** on?

**No one likes
a spider bite,**
*but don't you think
the spider might?*

Are crabs **befuddled** when plans **get scuttled?**

If mud in a puddle **makes it muddled,**

do kiddie pools become *piddled?*

Answers abound!

They can often be found by tossing around— you guessed it—

more **questions!**

Any suggestions?